ANNA BRANFORD

illustrated by

SAM WILSON

WALKER
BOOKS

This is a work of fiction. Names, characters, places and incidents are either the product of the author's imagination or, if real, are used fictitiously. All statements, activities, stunts, descriptions, information and material of any other kind contained herein are included for entertainment purposes only and should not be relied on for accuracy or replicated as they may result in injury.

First published 2010 by Walker Books Australia Pty Ltd

First published in the UK 2012 by Walker Books Ltd
87 Vauxhall Walk, London SE11 5HJ

2 4 6 8 10 9 7 5 3 1

This book has been typeset in Bembo

Printed and bound in Great Britain by Clays Ltd, St Ives plc

British Library Cataloguing in Publication Data:
a catalogue record for this book is available from the British Library

ISBN 978-1-4063-2693-2

www.walker.co.uk

www.violetmackerel.com

Violet Mackerel's Brilliant Plot

Other Violet Mackerel stories to collect:

Violet Mackerel's Remarkable Recovery

To Sylvia (my granny)

AB

To George and Molly

SW

The Red Button

Violet Mackerel is a girl with a theory. Her theory is that when you are having a **very important** and brilliant idea, what generally happens is that you find something small and special on the ground.

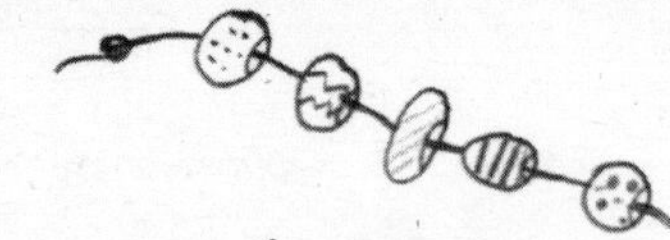

So whenever you spy a sequin, or
a stray bead, or a bit of ribbon,

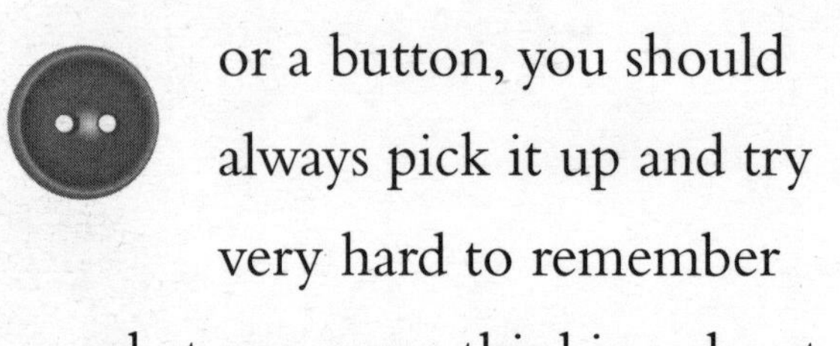

or a button, you should
always pick it up and try
very hard to remember

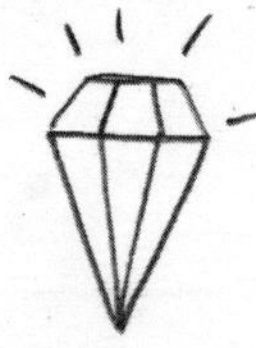

what you were thinking about
at the precise moment

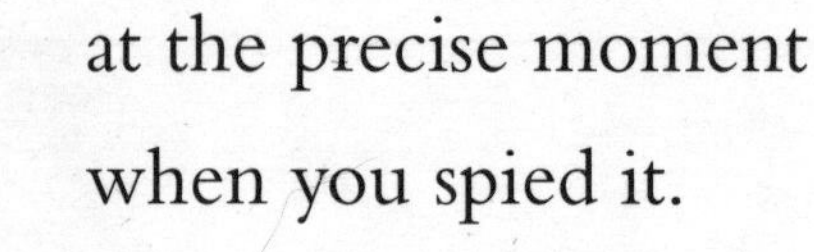

when you spied it.
Then think about that
thing a lot more.

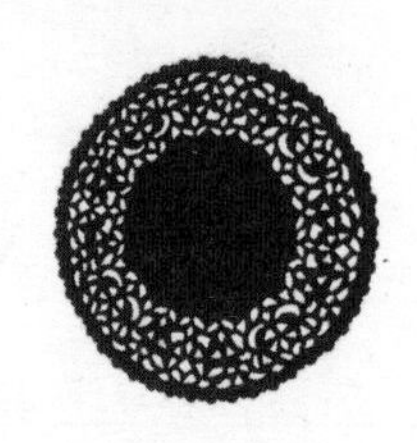

That is Violet's theory,

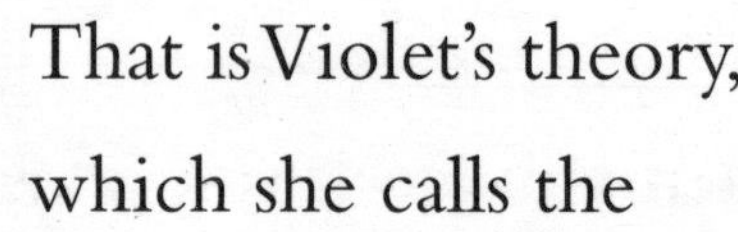

which she calls the

Theory of
Finding
Small
Things.

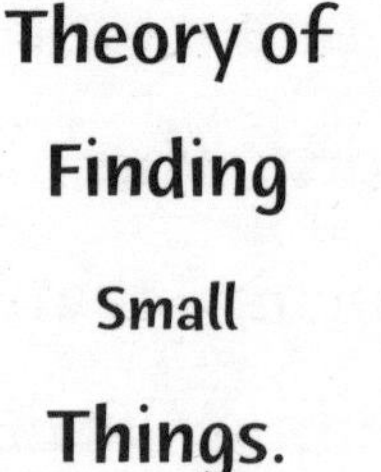

"Wake up, Violet," says Violet's mum. "It's nearly five o'clock."

It is Saturday, which is market day. Violet yawns. It is still dark. Mum's hair is a bit damp from her shower and it smells like mangoes and blossoms. Violet leans forward for a snuggle and nearly falls asleep again.

"Just stay awake until we're all in the van," says Mum. "Then you can sleep as much as you like."

Violet's big brother, Dylan, and big sister, Nicola, are already awake and they are helping to load up the van with fold-up tables and chairs, the big canopy umbrella, and boxes and baskets of Mum's knitting. They are going to the market like they do every Saturday morning, to sell the woolly things Mum makes.

Violet thinks she would quite like to wear her pyjama bottoms under her skirt today. They feel nice and warm from bed. Sometimes if you say things like "Can I wear

my pyjama bottoms to the market?",
people say things like "No." But if
you just put your skirt on over the top,
and have your eyebrows slightly raised
like someone who is thinking of
something **very important**
and interesting,
no one says
anything at all.

When Violet, Mum, Nicola and Dylan arrive at the market, even though it is still not properly light, lots of people are already there, rugged up

and rubbing their hands together with coldness, unfolding and unpacking their things to sell. No one notices Violet's pyjama bottoms.

Violet's favourite person at the market (apart from Mum and Dylan and Nicola and herself) is a man who never smiles. He sells china birds, small enough to fit in the palm of your hand, and he is there every week. Violet says hello to him as she always does, and he doesn't even look up, which he never does. But after waking up at nearly five o'clock in the morning, Violet doesn't feel much like chatting or smiling either. So she feels that even though he never says hello back, she and the man might share a sort of **understanding**.

The man's china birds are all different and all very dirty. Dylan says that they are probably brand-new from a factory. He thinks the man has just put dirt on them so they will look ancient and he can sell them for ten pounds instead of two. But Violet doubts it. She thinks it is much more likely that he is an **archaeologist**. She suspects that he specializes in digging up ancient china birds.

Violet would quite like to own one of the man's birds in particular. It is made of pale blue china, the colour of a robin's egg. It is always right at the back of the table.

And just as she is having that thought, out of the corner of her eye, Violet spies a small red button on the dusty market ground.

The Important Idea

Violet picks up the red button.

She puts the button in her pyjama pocket, hidden by her skirt. It is a safe and secret place.

"Right when I spied that red button," she says to herself, "I was thinking of how much I would like to own that BLUE CHINA BIRD. So now I know," thinks Violet, "that it was not just a silly wish but a **very important** idea."

However, the bird is ten pounds and Violet does not have ten pounds. Violet does not even have one pound.

Violet thinks.

It is quite nice to hear the noisiness and busyness of the market growing as more and more people start to arrive, but it can be a bit distracting when you are trying to have a brilliant idea. So Violet gets a blanket and a cushion out of the back of the van and makes herself a sort of nest in the back seat. From her nest, Violet can still see what is going on at the market, and she can think more clearly.

It is all right for Violet's sister, Nicola. She is a teenager and all she wants is a haircut by a person called Mojo who only works at a particular hair salon on Wednesdays.

Nicola has made earrings with wire and pliers. She is arranging them on the same table as Mum's woolly things.

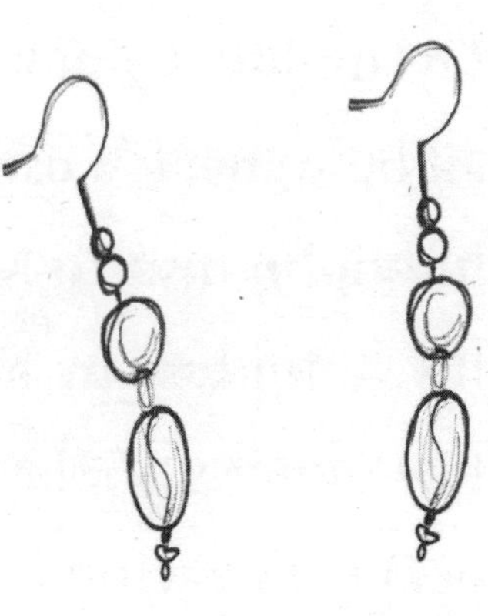

She is pinning them to a corkboard with a sign saying

Violet likes Nicola's earrings and she thinks quite a few people will probably want to buy them.

It's also all right for her brother, Dylan. He is almost a teenager and all he wants is a camera. He is playing his violin next to Mum's stall with his violin case by his feet, and every few minutes Violet hears the jingle of people throwing coins into it.

Dylan only knows three songs, and one of them is a Christmas song, and it won't be Christmas for a very long time. But no one at the market seems to mind and he is getting quite a few coins to save for his camera.

When you only want something ordinary, like a camera or a haircut, you only need an ordinary plan, like playing the violin or making earrings. But if what you want is something **really, really important**, and if the importance has been proven by your **own personal theory**, then ordinary plans are no good.

What you need is a *plot*.

A *brilliant* plot.

Fortunately, Mum keeps a notebook in the van and she doesn't mind people plotting in it. Violet reaches over to take the notebook and a pen out of the glove compartment and then rearranges her nest so she can rest the book on her knees. This is what she writes

Then it is just a matter of thinking

what

to

write

next.

The Thinking Box

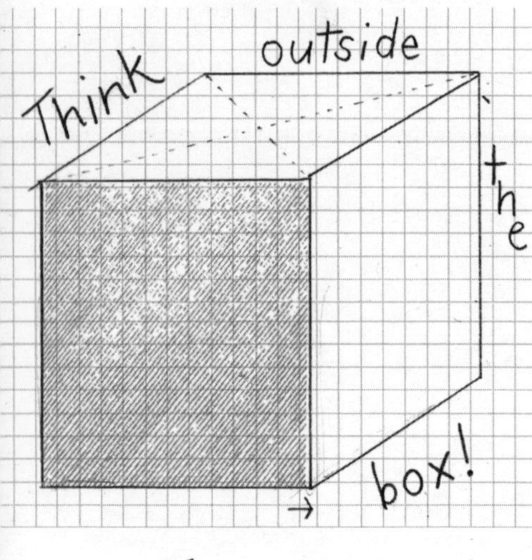

Mum sometimes says that it is quite helpful, when you are trying to solve a difficult problem, to **think outside the box**.

Outside-the-box thinking is how Mum thought of doing knitting when Dad left and she was feeling sad.

People made suggestions like

"Perhaps you could try jogging in the mornings"

and

"Why don't you take an evening class?"

But those are inside-the-box sorts of ideas, and not much good for people like Mum.

Knitting is different.

The blanket Violet is nesting in was one of the first things Mum ever knitted. She made it especially for Violet – soft and feathery brown– because Violet

likes small brown sparrows, and she added some purplish patches because actual violets are purple. It is Violet's favourite blanket.

Knitting makes Mum happy and relaxed, even when the phone is ringing and there is someone at the door, and Dylan is yelling at Nicola, "IF YOU DON'T GET OUT OF THE BATHROOM NOW, I WILL TELL ANGUS PODMORE THAT YOU LOVE HIM," and Nicola is nearly crying because she still has conditioner in her hair and she *can't* come out. So Violet thinks that knitting was quite a good idea of Mum's.

Violet decides she might try the trick

of thinking outside the box. So she crosses out the part in her notebook where she has written "**Actual plot**" and instead she draws a big thinking box. Inside the box she writes ordinary ideas, such as

When the box is full of very ordinary ideas, she writes her interesting ideas outside it.

These are things like

Violet likes these ideas, especially the ones outside the box, but she feels that she has not yet stumbled upon a **brilliant plot**. These are all only **quite good plots**.

Violet must have been thinking and plotting for a while and maybe even falling asleep a little bit (which is easy to do if you have made a very comfortable and warm nest), because Mum opens the van door and says, "Are you all right in there?"

"Yes," says Violet. "I'm just doing some plotting."

Violet decides to take a break from plotting because Mum has bought everyone some little pancakes called **poffertjes**. They come in a paper cup with a drizzle of maple syrup and a long pointy wooden skewer to spike them with. They are one of Violet's favourite things.

Violet sits by the knitting stall with Mum and Nicola and Dylan and they all spike at their poffertjes and get a bit sticky. And just as Violet is thinking about stickiness, and not actually about plotting at all, a funny thing happens. The beginning of a **brilliant plot** suddenly sprouts in her mind.

When she has finished her last poffertje, Violet crawls underneath the table of Mum's knitted things. She is hidden by the tablecloth hanging down so no one can see what she is doing. Using the pointy wooden skewer from her poffertjes, she begins to scratch in the dirt. The top layer crumbles easily away, so Violet digs some more, scooping the dirt into a little pile beside the growing hole with her hands.

"What are you doing?" asks Mum after a while, peeking under the tablecloth.

"Being an **archaeologist**," says Violet.

A **good plot** is now settling properly in Violet's mind. If she finds something very precious, like an ancient jewel or a rare dinosaur bone, she will become rich and famous for her discovery. Then she will be able to buy the BLUE CHINA BIRD. It would be good to find even a very small thing, just to be sure the idea is an important one, but so far there is just more dirt.

Violet scratches and scoops under the table. She doesn't find any ancient jewels or rare dinosaur bones.

She takes the red button out of her hidden pyjama pocket and buries it in the dusty dirt.

Finding things you have hidden yourself isn't quite as much fun as finding proper treasure,

but it is much better than finding nothing.

Soon Mum is ready to pack up the stall and Nicola is saying that if she hears Dylan's Christmas carol one more time, she will chop off her own head.

Violet has not found any treasure. She hasn't even found anything ordinary, like a paperclip or a bottle top.

Just the red button, over and over again.

But she is not ready to give up just yet.

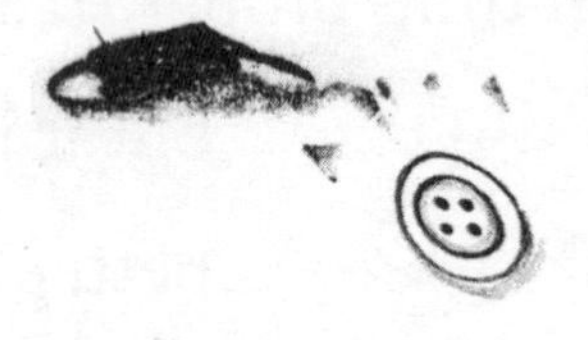

The Mind's Eye

That afternoon when they get home, Violet's mum does her French lesson. She is learning from a set of CDs and a book.

"Red!" says the man on the CD.

"Roooooosh," says Mum.

"Green!" says the man on the CD.

"Vairrrrrr," says Mum, as if she has a hair in her mouth.

Mum has been trying lots of new things lately. Stuck to the wall in the kitchen is a small piece of paper on which she has written the words

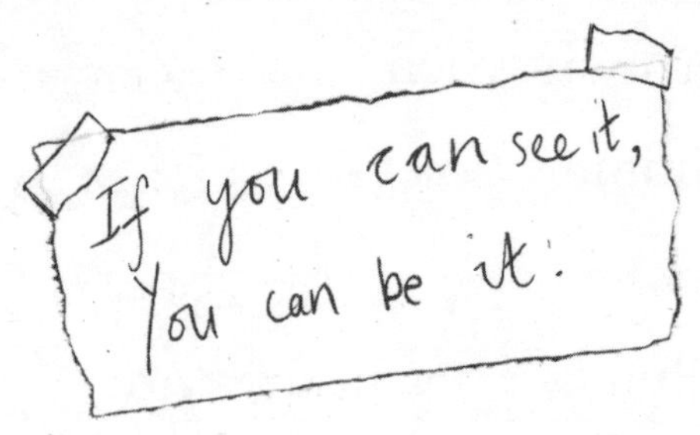

After Dad left, a few of these bits of paper started to appear around the house.

"Is that your theory?" Violet asks.

"Sort of," says Mum.

"What does it mean?" asks Violet.

"I think it means that if you can picture something very clearly in your **mind's eye**, you can make it happen."

Violet quite likes the idea that her mind has an eye.

"What does your **mind's eye** see?" Violet asks.

"Well, first, I see you and Dylan and Nicola growing up happy and healthy. And then when you are all grown up, I see myself in Paris, speaking French and maybe knitting scarves and leg warmers for a boutique or two," says Mum, squatting down to pick something up.

"What's that?" asks Violet.

"One of Nicola's earrings, I think," says Mum, putting it in her pocket, as Violet has explained the **Theory of Finding Small Things** to her before.

"If I am not quite grown up, can I come with you to Paris?" asks Violet.

"Yes," says Mum.

"And if I *am* properly grown up, I will send you postcards from my archaeological digs."

"I would like that," says Mum.

Violet goes to her room where she has taken her notebook of plots. At the top of the page she writes

If I can see it I can be it

Then she closes her eyes.

Her ***mind's eye*** sees all sorts of things, like herself on a talk show with the title "**Girl archaeologist discovers new dinosaur, to be named *Violetosaurus Mackerelus***".

The talk show host says to her, "So, Violet, how did you actually find the bone that led to this incredible discovery?"

"Well, Max," says Violet (since Max seems to be the name her ***mind's eye*** has given to the talk show host), "there was a BLUE CHINA BIRD at the market, and I was thinking outside the box about how I could get it..."

The studio audience says, "Ahhh!", because they think it is a nice sort of wish. But they are also amazed by her cleverness. They are all planning to send her china birds when they get home, so she will end up with hundreds of them. Probably all the talk show hosts will want to interview her after that. She might even be the richest and most famous dinosaur bone discoverer in the world.

Violet opens her eyes again. "**If I can see it, I can be it**," she says to herself.

Then she goes outside into the garden and the real dig begins.

The Archaeological Dig

The wooden skewer from the market was a good tool for digging under the table, but Violet suspects it is not the best tool for an **archaeologist**. There are proper spades and trowels in the garden shed which will make her job much easier.

There are even some old, soft paintbrushes, perfect for getting the very last of the dirt off precious treasure or old bones. And there might be all kinds of interesting things buried in the garden. Violet hopes there will even be a stray sequin glittering in the grass in the sun, to show her exactly where to dig.

Violet assembles her **archaeologist's** toolkit and when it is complete, she scans the garden for a sparkling hint. But there is nothing. So she decides to start right in the middle, where the grass is nice and soft. It looks like just the sort of place a dinosaur bone might be.

Violet digs and digs and digs. Sometimes she hits something hard (which always turns out to be a rock or a pipe, and not an ancient bone). Then she works on making the holes wider instead of deeper.

"**If I can see it, I can be it**," she says to herself.

As she digs, getting hotter and hotter and tireder and tireder, Violet makes sure she keeps on thinking about the ***Violetosaurus Mackerelus***. It will probably get in the newspaper, maybe even on the front page, as well as on Max's talk show. Then, when she is very rich and famous, Violet will buy Mum a whole rainbow of coloured wool. She will also buy Dylan a camera and Nicola a haircut by Mojo.

They will all say, "Violet, as well as being a brilliant plotter you are so generous, always thinking of other people and not of yourself."

(Although actually, first of all, she will buy herself the Blue China Bird.)

Suddenly, Violet hears a sort of coughing, gasping noise.

She looks up.

It is Nicola, and she doesn't look as though she is thinking of Violet's generosity. In fact, she looks more as if Dylan has been talking to Angus Podmore.

"What … are … you … doing?" she asks.

"I'm being an **archaeologist**," says Violet.

When she looks around her, though, she can see why Nicola's mouth is still a bit open. Their small back garden looks quite different

with so much of the grass the wrong way up.

"**Archaeologists** have to make a *little* bit of mess," says Violet. "Otherwise, they might never find any treasure at all."

"A little bit of mess?" Nicola gasps. "You've wrecked the garden!"

"I have not," says Violet, very crossly.

"You have so," says Nicola.

"Peabrain," yells Violet.

"Garden wrecker," yells Nicola back.

Then Mum comes out to see what all the fuss is about.

The Slight Disaster

"Oh, Violet," says Mum, putting both her hands over her mouth and then over her eyes. "What were you *thinking*?"

"I was thinking of a **brilliant plot**," says Violet in the crossest voice she has ever, ever used. Clearly, no one is being at all amazed by her generosity.

Somehow the discovery of ***Violetosaurus Mackerelus***, the talk show and the newspaper, the rainbow of wool, the camera, the haircut by Mojo and even the BLUE CHINA BIRD seem to swirl and drain away like dirty bathwater.

Violet runs to her room and flops on the bed and howls and howls and her pillow gets wetter and wetter.

After a little while, Mum comes in and sits down on the bed next to her.

"Nicola said you were being an **archaeologist** again," says Mum.

"Yes," says Violet, into the pillow.

"There isn't any treasure in the back garden," says Mum.

"How do you know?" asks Violet, still into the pillow.

"Your dad and I shovelled that dirt there ourselves when we first bought the house, before you were born."

"Nobody ever tells me *anything*," says Violet, wondering what other important information they have all been keeping a secret.

"Maybe you could have asked before

digging up the garden," says Mum.

Then there is more howling, followed by lots of hiccups and a difficult time talking.

Mum's hair still smells a bit like mangoes and blossoms. It is nice, when you are having a slight disaster, to smell something like that.

Violet says, "My ***mind's eye*** got it wrong."

"Mine sometimes does that too," says Mum.

"What do you do when your ***mind's eye*** gets it wrong?" asks Violet.

Mum thinks.

"Wait a bit and then try something different," she says.

Then Violet gets her notebook and she and Mum think outside the box together about the garden.

Mum looks out the window where the soft patch of grass was. She says she has always wanted a Japanese sort of garden, perhaps with a fish pond and lots of white pebbles. Violet quite likes the idea of a fish pond but she thinks white pebbles might not be very nice to lie on in the sunshine, which is one of the things she likes to do when the weather is warm.

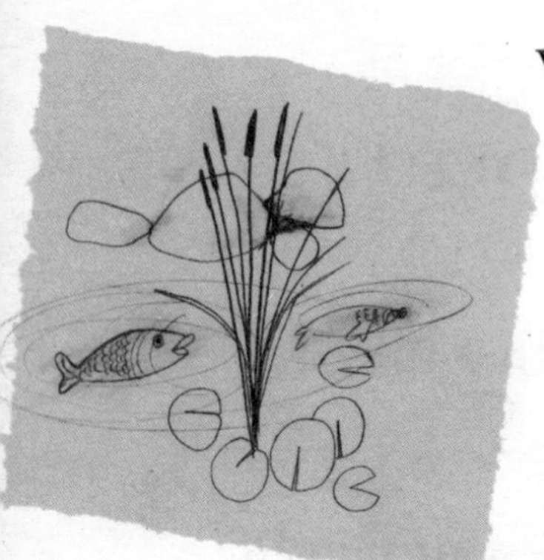

Violet says she likes farm animals and has always rather wanted a farm, perhaps with some chickens, a sheep and a smallish cow, which would eat all the leftover

grass so the holes would not be so noticeable. Mum says she quite likes farm animals too, but not necessarily in her own garden, since keeping a farm is a lot of work and also the neighbours might complain about all the clucking and mooing.

So in the end they decide to go to the plant nursery and buy a packet of bulbs, since the earth has been freshly turned and it is actually just the right time of year for planting them. Even though it is getting late by the time they get home, they neaten up the holes in the grass and plant the big, knobbly seeds in the soft, brown soil.

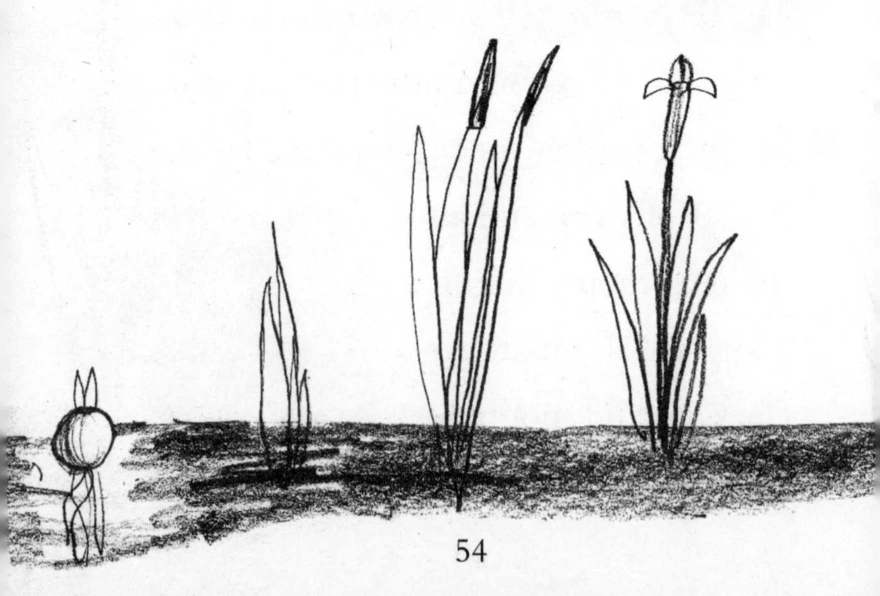

Violet is still disappointed, of course. It would have been much better to find some treasure or an ancient dinosaur bone, and to have been on a talk show, and best of all for the BLUE CHINA BIRD to be nesting on the table next to her bed. But even so, she quite likes thinking of daffodils and jonquils starting to grow where the treasure was supposed to be.

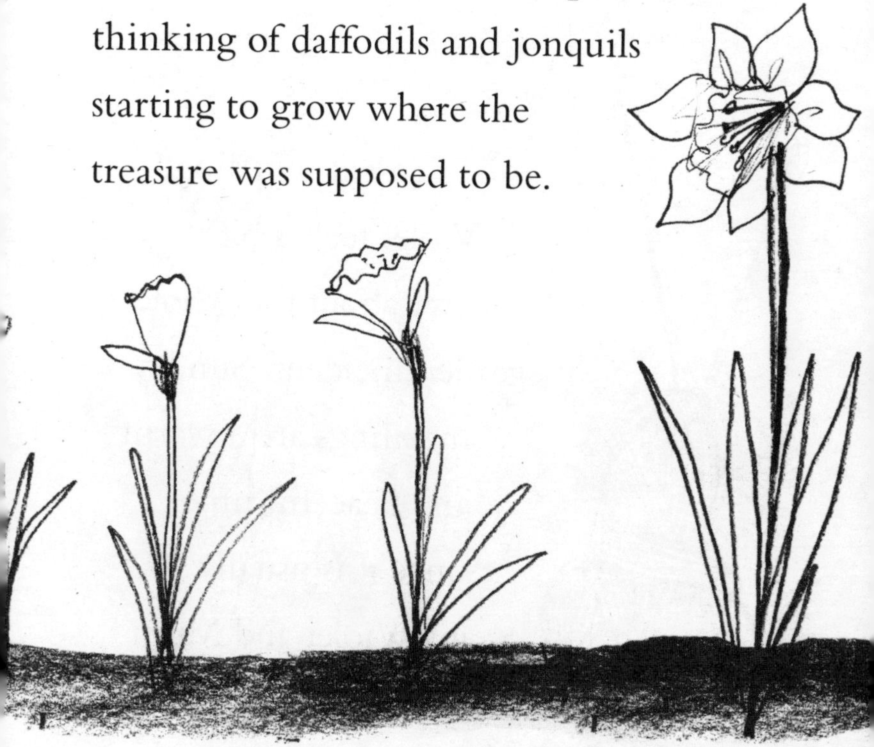

The Leg Warmer

The next morning, Violet feels a bit better about the whole garden incident. Sunday mornings are a warm and peaceful time, since it is usually just Violet and Mum because Nicola has netball practice and Dylan has chess. Mum sits close to the radiator and does knitting and Violet sits near by, doing a puzzle.

"What's that going to be?" asks Violet, seeing the purple and blue wool weaving together like colours in a sunset.

"A bag," says Mum.

Violet watches Mum knitting. It doesn't look too hard.

The **archaeology** plot did not work out quite as brilliantly as she had hoped, but Violet has not forgotten the BLUE CHINA BIRD and her mind's eye is looking out for some new ideas.

"Can I learn to knit?" asks Violet.

"Of course," says Mum, "when you're a bit older."

"I was thinking more like now," says Violet.

"Knitting is complicated," says Mum.

"I *like* complicated things," says Violet.

Mum has some knitting needles which are good for a beginner. While she is finding them, Violet does some more plotting in her notebook. The plotting is mostly a picture of some woolly cats and trousers and smallish trees and other things she might quite like to knit.

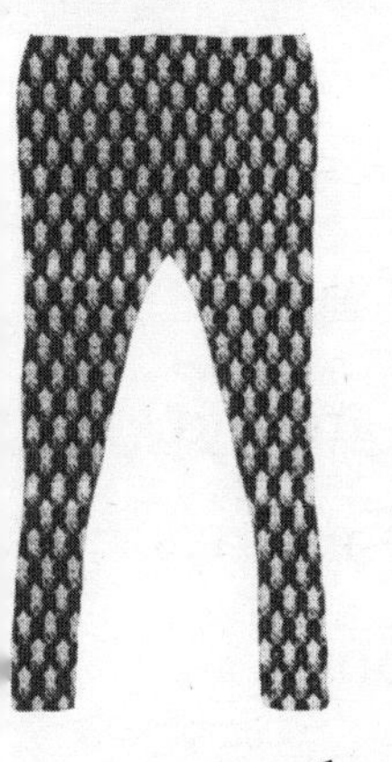

Then maybe she could have her *own* stall at the market, right next to Mum's, and earn enough money to buy the Blue China Bird.

(Also, she might be the first person in the world ever to have actually knitted a small tree, so she might get to be on a talk show, after all).

Mum comes back with the needles and casts on some thick green wool for Violet.

"Now," says Mum. "You put the needle through, loop the wool around, bring the back needle forward, and flick the stitch off. Through, loop, forward and flick. Through, loop, forward and flick."

It turns out that two needles and a ball of thick green wool are a lot for two hands to manage, even before you start looping and flicking.

Mum fixes up the bit where most of the casting on got cast off.

"Have another try," says Mum. "Through, loop, forward and flick."

Still it does not quite work.

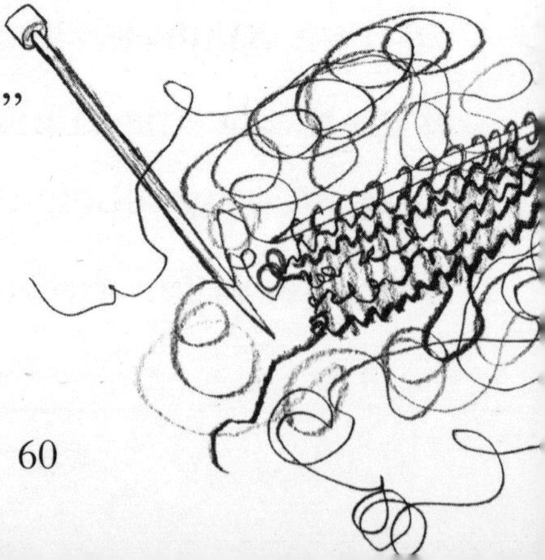

Through, loop, re-loop and twist.

Through, doesn't look right, turn over and strange knot.

Try to undo, drop, forget which needle and get cross.

Mum does not have her look of Sunday morning peacefulness any more. She has more the look of when the toaster has made the smoke alarm go off and no one can find the car keys and Nicola is saying that she is the only person at her whole entire school who does not have a mobile phone.

"Knitting is a difficult thing to learn," says Mum. "That box is full of my mistakes."

Violet puts down the knitting needles and wool and looks in the box. Inside it are some woolly squares with slight holes in them, scarves which are not at all long enough, some socks which stop around the toes and one short wide tube with some big loose patches. It is made of lots of odds and ends of wool, all different colours, with spidery threads hanging from it. Violet quite likes the woolly tube, so she pulls it out of the box.

"What's this?" asks Violet.

"It was going to be a leg warmer," says Mum, but I dropped a stitch or two and anyway it is much too loose for a leg."

"Both my legs go in it easily." Violet tries it on. "With arms in too," she says.

"Exactly," says Mum.

Violet

goes up

to her room

and brings down

a box of threads and ribbons

and buttons and sequins, beads and

other things she has spotted while

having important ideas.

The first thing she chooses is a green sequin that fell off the sparkly cardigan Mum wore every day last winter. She pushes one of the loose ends of the leg warmer through the middle of the sequin and ties a knot in the end to hold it in place. Then she starts the job of threading something from her box onto every loose end, weaving

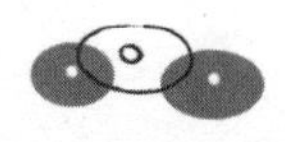

the dangling threads backwards and forwards through the knitting until they almost disappear.

While she is sitting on the floor and working on the leg warmer, Violet spots under a chair one of the little gold links Nicola uses for her earrings.

Violet carefully weaves the small thing in with the other treasures.

Even though the leg warmer wasn't exactly part of her plot, perhaps it is part of an **important idea** anyway.

The Tubular Scarf

Every day after school that week, Violet works on the leg warmer. Slowly, it gains more colours and dangles, beads and bits and sparkles.

On Friday, Violet threads on the red button she found at the market.

It is a bit muddy from being buried and found so many times, but you can still see a lot of the redness. It is a very good final touch.

"Can I put it on the table at the market in the morning?" asks Violet.

"Yes." Mum smiles. "What will you call it?"

Violet thinks.

"It is called a ***Tubular Scarf***," she says. "It works like this."

She puts the leg warmer over her head and bunches it around her neck to show Mum. It fits loosely like a scarf.

"Plus you can do this," says Violet, pulling the back part over her head like a medieval hood.

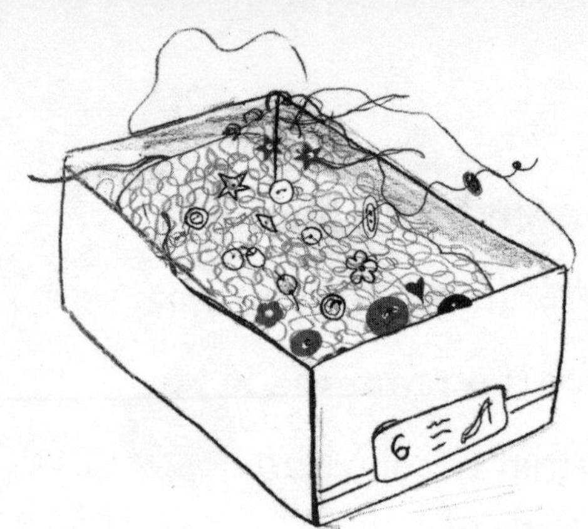

Violet asks Mum for a shoebox to put the scarf in. But on the Friday night before the market, when the time has nearly come to put it inside and shut the lid, Violet finds that she would actually rather not.

If someone buys the ***Tubular Scarf***, then maybe she will have enough money to buy the BLUE CHINA BIRD, which is **very important**. But Violet wonders if the person who buys it will know that it can be both a scarf and a hood. She wonders if they will notice all the small things woven into it, especially the red button. They might not realize that the scarf was made partly by her and partly by Mum. And all of those things are actually quite important too.

"Mum, do you ever secretly hope that people don't buy your knitted things, so you can keep them a bit longer?" Violet asks.

"Sometimes I decide I don't want anyone to buy them at all," says Mum, "so I keep them or give them to you or Nicola or Dylan."

"Giving things is different from keeping them or selling them," says Violet.

"Sometimes it's nicer," says Mum.

Nicola only needs to sell two pairs of earrings tomorrow and then she will have enough money to visit Mojo on Wednesday.

Dylan needs a bit more for his camera than he will probably get from playing his violin tomorrow, but he is still hopeful.

Violet suspects it is all quite easy if what you want is something quite ordinary, like a haircut or a camera. Then you just do ordinary things, like making earrings or playing the violin. But the BLUE CHINA BIRD is a different *sort* of thing. That is the problem.

Violet writes on the lid of the shoebox with a purple marker.

Tubular scarf made partly by Violet Marckerel, £10

Then she puts the scarf in the box. But for quite a long time she leaves the lid off.

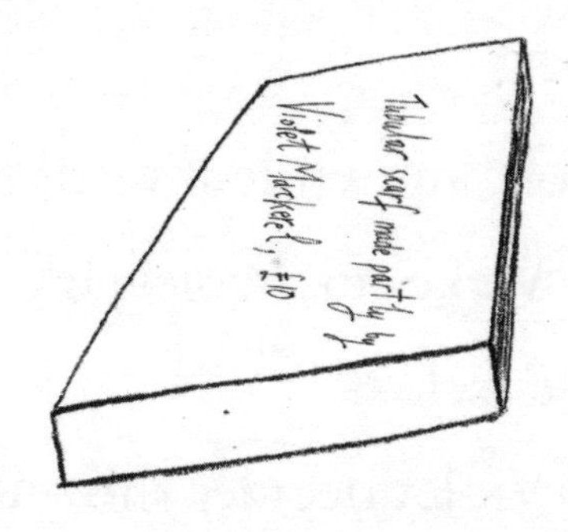

The Smiling Man

The next morning while it's still dark, Mum says, "Wake up, Violet. It's nearly five o'clock."

Violet decides she will wear her pyjama bottoms to the market again, since last week she was especially nice and warm.

Nicola and Dylan help Mum carry things out to the van and Violet carries the box with the ***Tubular Scarf***.

She keeps the box on her lap all the way to the market.

When they arrive Violet helps set up the stall.

"I'm not going to put the **Tubular Scarf** out just yet," she says to Mum. "First I think I will go for a small walk."

Violet walks over to the stall of the man who doesn't smile, so she can look at all the colours of the china birds on his table and check that the BLUE CHINA BIRD is there.

It is **not**.

The man is busy rummaging in his van so Violet looks carefully at every bird again, just to make sure. Mum says it is best not to worry until you are quite sure there is something to worry about. But now Violet has checked.

It is *definitely* not there.

"Did somebody buy the BLUE CHINA BIRD?" asks Violet, who has a very uncomfortable feeling growing in her chest.

The man does not turn around.

"DID SOMEBODY BUY THE BLUE CHINA BIRD?" Violet asks, much more loudly.

"Did you say something?" asks the man who doesn't smile.

And he smiles at Violet!

"Sorry, I am a bit deaf," he says.

"I asked you about the Blue China Bird," says Violet, whose heart is bumping around inside her. "The one that is about the colour of a robin's egg."

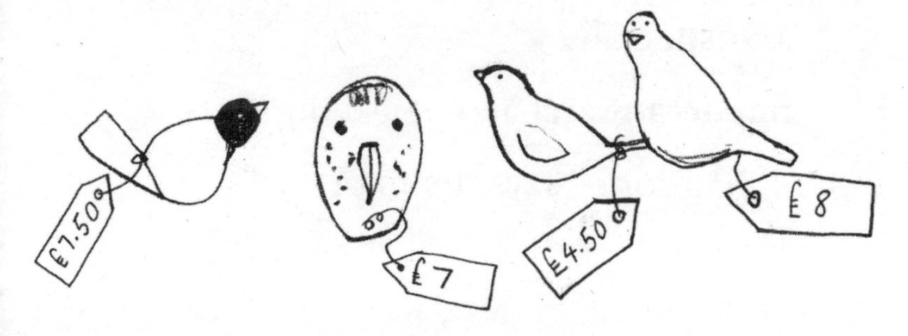

"Oh, *that* one," he says. "I always unpack that bird last of all, because secretly I hope no one will buy it. It's my favourite."

The man takes the beautiful bird gently out of its scruffy newspaper packaging and puts it on the table. Gradually, Violet's chest goes back to normal.

"It's my favourite too," says Violet. "Did you find it on an **especially important** archaeological dig?"

"Pardon?" says the man.

"You are an **archaeologist**, aren't you?"

"No," says the man.

"What are you then?" asks Violet.

He thinks for a bit.

"A backpacker," he says. "I bought my china birds from a potter who I met when I was backpacking in Spain last year."

Violet thinks how nice grey eyes are with a green jumper, which is what the man has. But he looks as if he needs a jacket too. He is rubbing his hands together and blowing on them.

"You look cold," says Violet.

"Backpackers don't mind the cold too much," says the man, whose name turns out to be Vincent.

"The best thing for coldness," Violet tells him, "is to keep your pyjama bottoms on under your clothes. Hardly anyone notices."

"Really? I might try that next week," he says.

A thought is coming into Violet's mind. If smiling Vincent had a ***Tubular Scarf***, he could be nice and warm this week.

And just as she is thinking it, she spies a small stray piece of the coloured string Vincent uses to put paper tags on his birds. It has blown underneath the table.

Vincent says she can keep it, so Violet picks it up and puts it in her pocket.

Then she goes back to the van and gets out the shoebox with the scarf inside. She finds a pen in the glove compartment and scribbles out the part on the lid that says £10, but leaves on the part that says

She feels a bit shy going back.

"Hello again," says Vincent when he sees her. "What have you got there?"

"It's a **Tubular Scarf**," says Violet. "I partly made it."

"So I see," says Vincent, reading the box.

"Who made the rest?"

"My mum," says Violet.

"Is she the knitter a few stalls over?" asks Vincent.

"Yes," says Violet, "and she is also a learner of French."

"So am I," says Vincent. "In fact, I plan to go backpacking in France one day."

"Mum too," says Violet. "She sounds like she has a hair in her mouth."

"She *is* doing well then," says Vincent.

Violet opens the box and holds it out to Vincent. He takes the scarf out very carefully and tries it on. It fits him snugly and Violet thinks he looks warmer already. Then she shows him how you can also pull the back part up over your head like a medieval hood.

"What a good idea," says Vincent. "How much is it?"

"Nothing," says Violet. "It's a present."

Vincent smiles the nicest smile of all.

"I love it," he says. "I especially like the red button."

In a funny way, it is *almost* as good as having the BLUE CHINA BIRD, Violet thinks, to see him smiling and feeling warmer.

"Since your Mum partly made this, do you think she would mind if I stopped by later on to say thank you?"

"I don't think she would mind," says Violet.

When Vincent does stop by a bit later, he is still wearing the ***Tubular Scarf*** and he puts quite a lot of money in Dylan's violin case.

"Christmas carols are my favourite," he says.

Mum smiles.

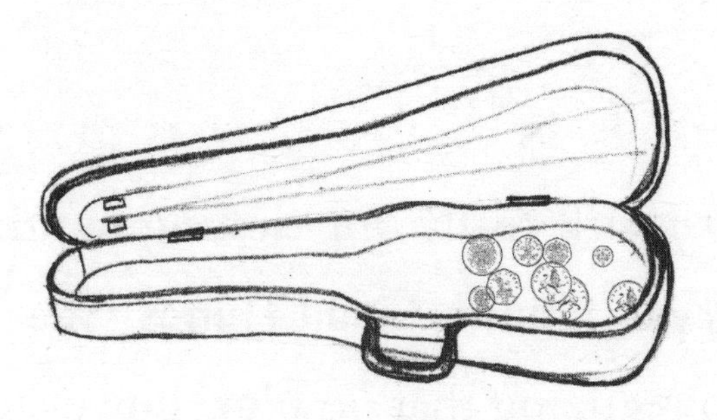

The Blue China Bird

Violet is still really only testing out the **Theory of Finding Small Things**. She is also realizing that no **plot**, however **brilliant**, can be absolutely sure to work.

But on Monday, Dylan has enough money to buy his camera and now he is busy all the time – too busy, even, to say anything to anyone about Angus Podmore when Nicola is taking a very long time in the bathroom. He is always out in the garden, photographing the growing bulbs which have little green shoots already.

And on Wednesday afternoon, not only does Nicola go to see Mojo at the hair salon, but Mum goes too,

and they both come home with coloured bits and straight bits and funny lengths at the back.

And that evening while Mum's hair is still special, Vincent comes round to eat a roast dinner and practise French. When he arrives he is wearing the Tubular Scarf, pulled up at the back like a medieval hood. They have to turn the volume up on the CD player as Vincent really is a bit deaf.

"Black!" says the man on the CD.

"Nwaaaaaar," says Mum.

"Nwaaaaaar," says Vincent, who now seems to smile all the time.

After dinner, while Mum and Nicola and Dylan are busy clearing away plates and putting sprinkles on ice-cream for dessert, Vincent takes something out of his pocket and gives it to Violet. It is wrapped in soft purple tissue paper. "What is it?" asks Violet.

"A present," says Vincent.

Violet carefully unravels the purple tissue. Then, even more carefully, she unravels the scruffy newspaper underneath.

And after that, Violet smiles the nicest smile of all. Because there in her hands, sitting in a soft nest of tissue and newspaper, is the BLUE CHINA BIRD.

How to Make a Box of Small Things

If you would like to make a box of small things like Violet's, it is quite easy to do.

1. The first thing you will need is a box.

The size and sort is up to you. An empty matchbox is handy because it will fit easily in your pocket, plus you can fit a surprising number of small things into a matchbox. A shoebox is also useful because you can fit even more small things in one of those. It all depends on what sorts of boxes are spare at your house.

2. The next thing is to make it very clear that this is not the sort of box that anyone should accidentally throw away,
which you do by labelling it.

You could write something like:

Juliet's Box of Small Things

or

Small Things Belonging to Lucy

or

These Small Things are the Property of Thomas.

3. The best boxes of small things tend to be decorated with *drawings*, perhaps of the sorts of small things you plan to put inside.

4. Then it is just a matter of searching for small things to put in your box. You might have some you have been keeping already. People in your family might even have one or two that they don't mind giving you. But if not, you can always go for a walk and see what you can find.

These are some of the things you could look out for:

Beads, buttons,

little bits of ribbon, paperclips,

hair slides, small coins, sequins,

pieces of lace, feathers,

leaf skeletons, bits of confetti,

stamps, coloured threads and strings,

small pebbles (especially if they

have an interesting shape),

pieces of tumbled glass,

charms, seashells, tiny crystals,

seed pods, marbles and

lost jigsaw puzzle pieces.

And don't forget, if you are lucky enough to spot one of these things when you are out walking, try to remember what you were thinking at the moment you spotted it. It might turn out to be

a

very

important

idea.

Look for other ideas at:

www.violetmackerel.com

small things belonging to Molly
ONE PENNY
1
Love

ANNA BRANFORD was born on the Isle of Man, but spent her childhood in Sudan, Papua New Guinea and Australia. Once, when she was very itchy with the chicken pox, her dad read her *The Very Hungry Caterpillar* thirty times in a row.

Anna lectures in Sociology at Victoria University, Australia, and spends her evenings writing children's stories, kept company by a furry black cat called Florence. She also makes dolls using recycled fabric and materials.

SAM WILSON graduated from Kingston University in 1999 and has since been working on lots of grown-up books. The Violet Mackerel books are the first titles she has illustrated for children. She says, "I have always wanted to illustrate for children, it has been such fun drawing Violet, she is a gorgeous character with such an adventurous spirit." Sam lives in the countryside with her husband, two children, a black Lab called Jess and several chickens.